THE LADY AND THE RABBIT

The Shifter Season

LAURA GREENWOOD

© 2022 Laura Greenwood

All rights reserved. This book or parts thereof may not be reproduced in any form, stored in any retrieval system, or transmitted in any form by any means – electronic, mechanical, photocopy, recording or otherwise – without prior written permission of the published, except as provided by United States of America copyright law. For permission requests, write to the publisher at "Attention: Permissions Coordinator," at the email address; lauragreenwood@authorlauragreenwood.co.uk.

Visit Laura Greenwood's website at:

www.authorlauragreenwood.co.uk

Cover by Ammonia Book Covers

The Lady and the Rabbit is a work of fiction. Names, characters, places, and incidents are the products of the author's imagination or are used fictitiously. Any resemblance to actual persons, living or dead, businesses, companies, events, or locales is entirely coincidental.

If you find an error, you can report it via my website. Please note that my books are written in British English: https://www.authorlauragreenwood.co.uk/p/report-error.html

To keep up to date with new releases, sales, and other updates, you can join my mailing list via my website or The Paranormal Council Reader Group on Facebook.

Blurb

Denise Foxe doesn't have the same interest in the Season as her sister does, she'd much rather read a book than dance with eligible suitors.

When she meets a handsome rabbit shifter who seems to share her interest in reading, she finds herself willing to break all of society's rules in order to spend more time with him.

Can they continue their affair without risking getting caught?

-

The Lady and the Rabbit is a paranormal Regency romance with fox and rabbit shifters. It is a Shifter Season short story. It has an m/f romance and is Denise and George's complete story.

Chapter 1

DENISE

As little as I wish to be at a ball such as this, I have to admit that the music is a divine accompaniment to my book, and is definitely preferable to Victoria's playing of the pianoforte. Not that she is bad, but it is rather distracting to have her play a note wrong when I am deep in the most dramatic parts of my book.

The song comes to an end, and the chatter of excited voices replaces it as the many people on the dancefloor change.

Out of curiosity, I set down my book and lean over the balcony, trying to find my twin amongst the dancers.

It only takes me a moment, but I spot her opposite a dark-haired man who looks vaguely familiar.

He turns to her and I catch sight of his face. Ah, Viscount Renarton. The fox shifter next door who Victoria was always getting into trouble with when we were all children.

Even from here, I can sense my sister's amusement and a small smile crosses my face. They always got along well, and it is nice to see her in the presence of a friend.

I search for Mama, though I do not see her amongst the crowd. I must admit to feeling a sense of relief at her style of chaperoning. When I was younger, I used to fear that she'd constantly be breathing over our shoulders and would never give either of us a chance to actually make a connection with anyone. Thankfully, that doesn't seem to be the case.

Satisfied that no one is going to pay me any attention, I pick up my book and start reading again.

I soon lose myself in the English countryside alongside the headstrong heroine who refuses to just marry because she should. I envy her for the choice, even if she isn't real.

"Oh, I must apologise, I didn't realise there was someone up here," a voice says.

I startle, dropping my book in the process.

"Allow me," the man says, bending down to retrieve it. He hands it back to me, and I take it. "Here."

"Thank you, My Lord."

Confusion flits over his face. "I'm not lord," he assures me.

"I find it is always wise to be cautious in situations like this," I respond. "If you were a lord, you would not be insulted because I addressed you as I should. As you are not, you are merely surprised."

"That is an astute observation, Miss..."

"Denise Foxe."

"It is a pleasure to meet you, Miss Foxe." He dips his head.

"Will you not tell me your name?"

"My apologies. I am Mr George Beaumont."

"Would you like to sit, Mr Beaumont?" I gesture to the seat beside me, knowing that I shouldn't be offering for him to sit so close to me, especially with no one else here to witness what is happening.

"If you are certain, Miss Foxe. I don't wish to disturb your peace."

"And yet you already have." I offer him a small smile so he knows I am only jesting.

He lets out an amused chuckle. "You may have a point."

"So, will you join me?"

He nods and takes a seat.

"Why are you up here?" I ask.

"In truth, I am not a particular fan of dancing," he admits. "But with so many eager young ladies wishing to take part in this evening's festivities, I felt it was best to hide myself away."

"That isn't very gallant of you."

"Perhaps not, but sometimes, the world becomes too much, does it not?"

"What if I said I did not understand what you are talking about?"

"Then I would point out that you are up here reading your book, instead of down with the dancers."

"That is my sister's place. This is mine."

He raises an eyebrow. "Your sister?"

"You seem surprised that I have one, and yet you do not know me well enough to have such surprise."

"I suppose I am surprised."

"Whyever would you be?"

"If you do not care for dancing or partaking in the ball, why would your parents choose to present you when your sister is still unmarried?"

"How do you know she is not?"

"Married ladies do not participate in the dancing. Unless she is trying to cause a scandal, I have to assume she is there looking for a husband."

"How astute of you," I observe. "We are the same age, and were presented together."

"Ah. That is not a factor I had taken into consideration."

"Obviously."

"Is there a reason you do not like to dance?" he asks.

"I didn't say I didn't like it," I point out. "Merely that I would prefer to be here with my book."

"That is fair."

"But if you must know, I don't wish to dance because I do not see how it is possible to find a husband by dancing. Surely it should be done through the manner of proper conversation."

"I quite agree."

"Is that why you're hiding?"

"Partly. Though I will also admit that it is because I have grown weary of the shifters of the ton asking me what I am."

I raise an eyebrow. "You are a shifter?"

"I am."

"You shouldn't reveal such information when

you don't know whether your conversational partner is human or not."

"From your reaction, I can be certain you are not." He smiles, lighting up his boyishly handsome face. "But I had already suspected as much."

"There is no possible way for you to tell."

"Your book was a clue."

I glance down at it, but can't fathom how he could tell such information from the cover alone.

"I recognised the author. She is a shifter, is she not?"

"No one knows."

"But the subject matter of the book suggests as much."

"You seem remarkably well read for a gentleman," I note.

He raises an eyebrow. "You do not expect me to have read romance novels?"

"I believe many in your position would see them as a diversion unworthy of their attention."

"Then they must be living dreadfully boring lives."

I let out a small laugh, covering my mouth as I do. "I'm sorry, I don't mean to be improper."

"More improper than sitting away from the

dancing and reading romance books, you mean?" he teases.

"I won't apologise for it."

"And nor should you. I believe it is a most admirable use of your time," he says. "And it makes me wish to know you better."

"Then perhaps if you find yourself near my family home, you should call on me." Even I'm surprised by the suggestion, but I have to admit there's a sense of excitement lingering beneath them too. I don't know much about Mr Beaumont, but I want to learn more.

"I would be delighted, Miss Foxe, but I fear that may not be wise."

"Whyever would it not be?"

He glances away, his attention focused on the dancers beneath us. "I would not be a suitable match for someone of your status."

"You are a guest here, are you not?" I ask.

"At the ball?"

"Yes."

"Then I have every reason to believe that you are a suitable match. Certainly when it comes to conversation."

"I am not sure your family would agree. I don't have a title."

"Neither do I. My brother will inherit Papa's Barony."

"And I am not a fox shifter."

"I never said that I was a fox shifter."

"Ah, but you did confirm you were a shifter, and no one else would have the name Foxe," Mr Beaumont reasons.

"That is fair. But I don't see what you not being a fox shifter has to do with anything. My sister is down there dancing with all manner of shifters." I assume. The only person I've actually seen her dance with is Viscount Renarton, and I've seen him shift into his fox form with my own eyes.

Mr Beaumont lets out a sigh. "I'm a rabbit shifter."

"I don't see how that is of any importance to anything," I assure him. "When I am considering whether I wish to spend time with a gentleman, my first thought is to whether he can provide entertaining conversation, not what he can shift into."

Mr Beaumont nods. "If that is the truth, then it would be my pleasure to call on you."

A small smile spreads over my face, and satisfaction fills me at the idea of being able to continue our conversation.

"I must leave you to your book," Mr Beaumont

says, rising to his feet. "But I look forward to our future conversation."

"As do I." The smile I give him is genuine, and I hope he realises it.

"Miss Foxe." He bows to me, deeper than he needs to, but I like it.

"Mr Beaumont." I dip my head in return.

I watch him leave, a little disappointed that our conversation has had to come to an end already.

For a moment, I consider reopening my book and continuing to read, but if I don't return to the ballroom, I fear Mama will never forgive me.

I slip the book into my reticule, thankful I have one big enough, and make my way down the steps and into the ballroom properly. Time to do my duty and dance the way Mama would approve of.

Chapter 2

DENISE

Victoria's hands dance across the keys of the pianoforte, and I can tell from the confidence in the way she's playing, and the lack of wrong notes, that it's a piece she's comfortable with.

I turn the page in my book, enjoying the accompaniment.

She comes to a finish and folds her hands in her lap.

"That was pleasant," I say.

"I'm not disturbing your reading?" She frowns, as if seriously worrying about it. I hadn't realised she did.

"I find it soothing," I assure her. "Though if you were a worse player, then perhaps my answer would be different." It's a slight mistruth. She can be a terrible player at times, and then I would rather not be in the room.

"Then I will be grateful for the hours I've been granted to practise."

I let out a light laugh and glance towards the door. Should I tell her about Mr Beaumont? I'm not sure if he will actually follow through with his promise to call on me, but it would be nice to think that he would. "Are you expecting anyone to call?" I ask Victoria. She did much better at giving her attention to the right people at the balls.

"I don't think so. I'm supposed to be meeting Lord Leon for a promenade this afternoon though."

I let out a loud sigh, trying not to think about how much of a bore it's going to be. "I suppose I'm to be expected to come with you."

"Mama hasn't said, but I think she'll probably want you to."

"I suppose it's a chance to wear my new hat, I've been waiting for the perfect opportunity to."

"Does walking around the house not count?" An amused expression crosses her face, presumably as she recalls me wearing it after my purchase.

"You know it doesn't."

"Then I'm glad I've given you the perfect opportunity. Though perhaps it would be better if you waited until you had a suitor of your own to promenade with?" There's a note of expectancy in her voice, though I fear she's going to be disappointed.

"Is Mama really happy for you to promenade with Lord Leon? He can't be a serious suitor." I've never truly believed that my family would stand in the way of a match who wasn't a fox shifter, but it would be good to be certain of it.

"Because he's not a fox shifter?" Victoria checks, seeming to be thinking along the same lines as me.

I nod.

"I'll admit, it surprised me too, but he's handsome, has a decent reputation, and is the heir to a large fortune. I think that's enough for Mama to overlook one little issue," she says.

"And you?"

"I've never needed my match to be a fox shifter," she points out. "Though I thought that was what our parents would prefer."

"Me too, but I'm glad to hear they're open to something different, or else you'd end up married to Lord Renarton." I watch her face to see how she responds to the suggestion. She has no clue that I saw the two of them dancing.

"He's not that bad," she mumbles, glancing away from me as if she's hiding something. Perhaps she is, the two of them always used to get up to mischief. It wouldn't surprise me if they've managed now too.

"You haven't seen him in years," I say. "And last time we saw him, he stole my favourite ribbon to go fishing."

"He gave it back." An amused smile plays at her lips, revealing exactly what she really thinks of Viscount Renarton's boyhood actions.

"Ruined," I point out. Though I've long forgiven him for it.

"Anyway, he's in London. I saw him last night."

"You saw him?" I try to look surprised, and set down my book. Perhaps I should have admitted to seeing them together, but I feel she may tell me more about it this way.

"We danced."

"You shouldn't have wasted your time like that." He was perfectly pleasant as a boy, but I've heard rumours that suggest he may have grown up rather differently.

"It was just a dance," she counters. "Nothing will come of it."

"See that it doesn't."

"Why are you so against it?"

"I've heard things," I say vaguely.

"Like?"

"One of my friends said he shunned her at a ball and refused to dance with her."

Victoria grimaces, and for good reason. If the Viscount didn't already have a title, it would have been particularly bad for him to choose to do that.

We're saved from furthering our conversation by the double doors opening and one of the footmen stepping inside. "The Honourable Mr George Beaumont is here to see Miss Foxe," he announces.

My heart skips a beat. He's come. I don't think I believed it was going to happen until this moment.

Victoria glances in my direction, probably trying to work out if I know what is happening. A small blush rises to my cheeks and I look down at the floor, unable to form the words I need to.

"Show him in please, Varley," Victoria says once it becomes clear I have lost the ability to speak. "And please send for Mama, I'm sure she'll want to be present as chaperone."

I set my book to the side and start to smooth out my dress, wondering whether Mr Beaumont will think it is a pretty gown or not.

I dismiss the thought. He is clearly more interested in things other than what I'm wearing.

"Is there anything you want to tell me?" Victoria asks with a hint of a smile on her lips.

"No."

"Very well. Would you like me to sew or play the pianoforte?"

I think for a moment, though I don't need to. The answer is the option that will allow me to enjoy the company in the most peace. "The pianoforte, please."

"So Mama can't hear what you converse with Mr Beaumont about?" she half-teases.

"You're not going to leave this be, are you?"

"Probably not. You can either tell me now, or I'll be in your room after we retire and I'll pester you until dawn if you don't." Her threat is good-natured, but I have no doubt she'll see it through.

"Fine. But promise you won't tell Mama?"

Surprise flits across my twin's face. "What did you do?"

"Nothing scandalous," I assure her quickly.

"Then why are we not telling Mama?"

"Because we started talking about books at the ball the other day."

"And you don't think she'll find him a suitable match because of that?"

I let out a small sigh. "It's no matter. You don't understand."

"Denise, please? Tell me what's the matter."

"He's not a fox shifter."

"If that's not a problem for me, then it shouldn't be for you," she says kindly.

"Yes, but isn't your gentleman a lion shifter?"

"Well, yes." There's a reluctance in her voice that should have me threatening to bother her for the rest of the night.

"Then there's the problem," I say.

"I'm afraid I don't follow."

"He's a rabbit shifter."

"But you like him?" Victoria presses.

"I think so? We've only had one conversation, how much can I tell from that?" I won't be the fool who falls in love because of a single glance. I know better than that.

"True. But if you think you may come to like him more, then that's enough for me. We'll just have to keep it from Mama until after it's too late."

The conversation is ended by the doors opening. My heart skips a beat and I crane around to try to see Mr Beaumont, only to be disappointed when it's Mama who enters the room.

"A visitor is good news," she announces.

"Yes, Mama," Victoria says. "We're very excited."

"We should get into position," she instructs, looking between the two of us as if she wants to make all manner of adjustments to our gowns.

Victoria turns back to the pianoforte, and I feel a surge of affection for my sister. I'll have to make sure I repay her kindness should she have a caller she wishes to converse with in private. Though it will have to be in a way other than the pianoforte.

Mama makes herself comfortable on the chaise by Victoria.

My sister glances in my direction, presumably to make sure she's playing loudly enough. I give her the slightest of nods, grateful for her support.

"The Honourable Mr George Beaumont," Varley announces as he steps into the room.

Victoria pauses her playing, and the three of us dip our heads in acknowledgement of his entry.

"Miss Foxe, Miss Foxe, Lady Oxinforth." Mr Beaumont bows to each of us in turn. "It is a delight to be in your company."

"The pleasure is all ours," Mama responds. "Refreshments will arrive momentarily."

"Thank you." He smiles at me and makes his way over, sitting down beside me.

Mama raises an eyebrow, but doesn't say anything as she picks up her sewing. I don't need to ask to know that she isn't going to be paying much attention to where her threads are actually going.

"I have brought gifts." He holds out a small bundle.

Victoria begins to play, her fingers dancing over the keys as her tune fills the room.

"Thank you, that wasn't required, Mr Beaumont."

"I know. But I believe that refreshments are customary during meetings such as this."

"They are, but generally it is the host that provides them."

"Ah, and here is my thought. If you are the host, then I must assume that your favourite biscuits are being sent up from the kitchens. So I brought you my favourites so that we may both get to know one another better."

"And you believe we can do this with the exchange of biscuits?"

"Can we not?" he responds.

"I've never given someone's choice of biscuit to be particularly important," I admit.

"Perhaps not. But it is the kind of thing one

should know about people you wish to care for. Do you know your sister's favourite sweet?"

"She is partial to sugar plums," I say. "I suppose I do see your point. And I am grateful for the gift." I set the parcel on the side, looking forward to trying them later.

"It is a shame I could not bring you a book," he says. "I would very much have liked to share my favourites with you so we could discuss them."

"If you were to tell me the title of it, perhaps I could find a copy myself," I suggest. "Then the next time you call on me, we can discuss it."

"Would your family find that a proper topic of conversation?" he asks.

"My sister will not mind, though I suppose it is true that she won't be able to always play the pianoforte so loud in order to give us privacy."

"She is doing an admirable job."

"And one that I am certain is going to cause Mama to give her a stern talking to later." I glance briefly over to Mama, to find her looking rather unimpressed by the current situation.

"Perhaps I shall gift you a copy of the book at the next ball we are both in attendance of?" he suggests.

A small thrill shoots through me. I know I

shouldn't be accepting a gift as permanent as a book, nor should I be arranging to meet a gentleman at a ball. And yet, I can't help myself. For the first time, I find myself believing that I might possibly find a match to suit me.

I shouldn't let the first gentleman to show interest sweep me off my feet, but it is already becoming hard to imagine anyone else succeeding.

Chapter 3

GEORGE

A gaggle of young ladies stop their conversation as I pass them, whether because they do not wish me to overhear, or because they wish me to ask one of them to dance, I do not know.

Nor do I have any desire to find out. There is only one lady whose company I would accept on the dancefloor, and she luckily seems to have as much aversion to it as I do myself.

I make sure no one is looking and head for the stairs up to the balcony, a sense of excitement building inside me at the thought of seeing Miss Foxe again. So long as she is able to escape the notice of her chaperone and everyone else.

It isn't until I see the waiting lady that I relax.

"Miss Foxe." I bow deeply.

"Mr Beaumont."

Is it me, or is there a breathy note to her voice like she's as excited to see me as I am to see her? I certainly hope there is.

"May I join you?"

"Of course." She gestures for the seat by her. It doesn't escape my notice that she's not left very much room.

I sit down, my knee brushing against hers through the fabric of her dress.

"I have a new book for you," she says. "I'm sorry I could not bring yours back, I could only fit one in my reticule."

"I gave it to you as a gift, Miss Foxe, you don't have to return it."

A pleased expression dances through her eyes, but she covers it quickly. "It isn't a proper gift."

"Then it is an excellent thing that we are the only two people who know about it."

"Thank you," she says. "I particularly enjoyed the descriptions of the moors."

"Have you ever been?" I ask.

She shakes her head. "But I wish to."

"They are very beautiful," I respond. "I think you would like them."

"You've been?"

I nod.

"Did they match the way the author described them?"

"In the early mornings, they did," I tell her. "The mist lingers in the mornings and it makes it both eerie and peaceful at the same time. Like you are the only person in the world."

"That sounds wonderful." She gives a wistful sigh. "I wish I could see it, though I know it won't be possible."

"You could ask your husband."

"That would involve me finding one," she points out. "And considering I have successfully managed to spend the last three balls hiding on balconies with you, I don't believe that is going to happen any time soon."

I nod, while trying not to blurt out the suggestion that she should marry me. I know it is not the best suggestion to make given our different social statuses. She is the daughter of a wealthy baron, whereas I come from a not particularly wealthy branch of a family so far from a title that I will certainly never see it. I have never minded my lot in life as much as now I've met Miss Foxe.

"Will you be attending the ball on Friday?" Miss Foxe asks.

"Ah, I won't be. I have not received an invitation."

"Oh." She glances down at her lap. "I had hoped we could discuss the new book then."

"I can call on you, should you wish?"

She shakes her head. "Mama has insisted that Victoria shouldn't play the pianoforte when I have callers now. I believe she is punishing us for keeping our conversation private last time."

I let out an amused chuckle. "I'm surprised she didn't stop your sister from playing right then and there."

"I am too. If my sister hadn't already had a promenade with Lord Leon planned, I feel like she would have been in much more trouble for it."

"Lord Leon?"

"Yes. Do you know him?"

"More like *of* him," I respond, trying to keep the judgement out of my voice.

Miss Foxe raises an eyebrow. "What have you heard?"

"I don't believe it is my position to say."

"This is my sister, Mr Beaumont. Please, tell me what you know."

"I actually know very little," I say quickly. "It is

only vague rumours I have heard, but your sister should be careful."

"In truth, I do not believe she is particularly taken with him. I believe she is courting him because she believes that he would be a good match in our parents' eyes."

"Are your parents particularly set on good matches?" A part of me wishes I could avoid the question and live in denial that I could be considered an acceptable choice for Miss Foxe, but I know that won't be the case.

"No more or less than any of the other parents of young ladies our age," she responds. "But they are not as strict as some of my companions have mentioned their parents being."

"That must be a relief to you."

"An unimaginable one. I am certainly glad that Father has not secured an engagement for me without any input at all. It could be a far more dire situation for me this Season."

"And yet you have still decided to spend your balls on balconies with me discussing books."

"That is because your company is far superior to that of the rest of the gentlemen who wish to dance with me because they deem my face pretty enough, and my family wealthy enough. When I am with you, there is a reminder that I am more than just what I was born with."

"Then I am most glad that I can be of service to you, Miss Foxe."

"Denise," she says softly. "I believe it would only be right for you to call me by my first name."

"Then you must call me George."

"It would be my pleasure to. It suits you."

"Thank you." I dip my head.

"Denise?" a voice that sounds similar to hers calls up the stairs.

She lets out a small groan of frustration. "My sister," she says by way of explanation. "She must need me."

"Then we must say goodbye for now," I say. "Though I will miss your company."

"As will I." She pauses for a moment. "If you are not going to be at the ball on Friday, perhaps you should stop by my family home on Thursday?"

I raise an eyebrow. "To call on you?"

"That isn't quite what I had in mind," she admits. "I know it would not normally be considered proper, but I would be delighted to show you the family library, I think you'll enjoy the section Papa has allowed me to fill."

"If I am not to call on you officially, then how

would you plan on showing it to me?" I ask, trying not to get my hopes up for a meeting too much.

"How opposed would you be to shifting and hopping into a basket?" she asks.

I let out a low chuckle. "If there is a promise of time spent in your company at the end, then I believe it will be possible."

"Then I will send you a letter with instructions," she promises. "But I must go before Victoria finds us alone and begins to ask me questions neither of us can answer."

"It would be better if we can avoid them entirely," I agree, knowing that being alone with me could lead to Denise's ruin, even if neither of us wish it to.

"I shall await your instructions. Until Thursday, Denise." I rise from my seat along with her and dip into a bow, hoping she can sense how deeply it reflects my affections.

"I look forward to it." Instead of curtsying, she steps forward and presses a kiss against my cheek.

Before I can say anything about it, she hurries away, leaving me to touch my cheek and stare after her while standing in a mist of her perfume.

I know this is dangerous. We are playing with our hearts and in ways that we shouldn't.

And yet I can't seem to help myself.

Chapter 4

DENISE

I hurry down to the tree at the bottom of our garden, trying not to act like I'm doing anything suspicious. This is my home, and I'm allowed to be out here.

Though if anyone learns that the reason I'm out in the garden is because I plan on sneaking George into the house, then I may have to answer some questions I'm not ready for.

For a brief moment, I wonder why I'm doing this. It's such a risk, but the thought of not being able to see him at the ball on Friday filled me with such disappointment that I knew I needed to spend some time with him beforehand, and this is the best way I can come up with that will allow us to converse about what we wish to.

The Lady and the Rabbit

I just hope the two of us aren't going to get caught. I don't wish him to think that I invited him to my home in order to entrap him in anything.

I head towards the tree I told him to wait by, hoping he'll have listened to my instructions and be waiting there.

The afternoon sunshine warms me, promising an even more glorious day tomorrow. But that is of no matter right now.

I approach the tree and search around, wishing I'd thought to ask George what his rabbit form looks like lest I accidentally shepherd an unsuspecting creature into my basket instead of him.

"It's me," I say, just loud enough for him to hear if he's waiting.

A rustle comes from the bushes beside me, and I turn.

As expected, a large rabbit hops out and twitches his nose as he studies me.

Not knowing what to do, I dip into a curtsy. "Good afternoon," I say, placing my basket on the ground by him. A wild rabbit won't get into it, whereas George knows what I'm planning.

The rabbit looks over its shoulder at the bushes, which I take to be an indication of where his clothing lay.

A furious blush rose to my cheeks at the realisation that he won't be wearing any once he returns to his human form.

Perhaps I have not thought this through.

The rabbit hops into the basket and sits expectantly there, confirming that it is the object of my mission.

"Let me get your things," I say, heading to the bush and searching under it.

A neat pile of clothing, topped with a book, greets me. I pick up the pile and take it to the basket, placing the items carefully beside the rabbit.

"I need to close the lid, but we'll be in the library soon," I promise.

George nods his head. Or at least, I believe he does, it is hard to tell with such a form.

I close the lid of my basket and slip it over my arm. It's heavier than I expect it to be, but I don't have to carry it far.

I try to keep my pace steady so I don't attract the attention of any of the servants lest they tell my parents about this and raise questions I don't want to answer.

Or worse, if I encounter Victoria. My sister knows me better than anyone, and I fear that she

The Lady and the Rabbit

will be able to see through any lie I concoct. It is best that I stay away from her completely.

It only takes me a short while to get to the library, but by the time I get there, I'm starting to question the whole situation.

I set the basket down and take off the lid. "I was unable to get a screen for you to change behind," I say. "But I will be by the fire with my back turned until you tell me I can turn around."

The rabbit dips its head.

I take a few steps away and turn so I can fix my gaze on the flames in the grate instead of on the basket where the gentleman is changing back into his human form.

I know we shouldn't be doing this. There are a dozen reasons we shouldn't be alone together, and the family library is the last place I should have brought him either.

Something still lingers in the air, building with the promise of the conversation and connection to come. I want to ask him whether he is ready for me to turn around, but I fear that it would seem even more improper than the situation we've already found ourselves in.

That would also not be ideal.

"You may turn now," George says.

I let out a deep sigh and turn to face him, trying not to feel too disappointed by the fact he's fully dressed.

"I'm glad you came," I say. "Even if this does seem foolhardy."

"I believe that is part of the fun in an illicit meeting."

"Would you count this as illicit?" I ask, gesturing for the table I successfully set up with tea for two despite having to keep things from the servants.

"I believe any meeting in which the two of us would remain alone would be counted as illicit. You must know that my intentions towards you are honourable, despite the current situation."

"I know as much," I promise. "We are in the library and not my bed chamber." The moment the words are out of my mouth I realise how foolish they are, and yet I can not bring myself to retract them.

He raises an eyebrow. "Is that what occupies your mind?"

"Is it what you think of?"

George lets out a good-natured chuckle. "I thought that our afternoon would be focused on books."

"Oh." Disappointment fills my voice, but I'm not entirely sure where it comes from.

He steps closer. "What is the matter?" he asks. "I don't wish to disappoint." His voice is low and inviting.

I bite my bottom lip, trying to think of the best way to word my thoughts so he doesn't think I've invited him here to entrap him in anything untoward.

"Denise."

My name is almost too much to resist. "I suppose I was wondering why you haven't asked to kiss me yet." The words come out as nothing more than a whisper, but I'm certain he's heard them.

"Do you wish me to?" His voice isn't much louder than mine.

"I know it is not proper of me to admit it, but yes."

"Then this would seem like the perfect time," he says, closing the small distance remaining between us, but not reaching out to touch me just yet. "If anyone catches us here, then we will be in the same position whether we are to kiss or not."

"And you want to?"

He nods.

I reach out and cup his cheek in my hand,

feeling the anticipation for what's to come building up inside me. I didn't ever expect I would be in this situation when the Season started. If anything, I thought Victoria would be the one who got herself into a situation like this. Then again, with the way she keeps flirting with Viscount Renarton, perhaps she is too.

I banish thoughts of my sister from my mind and focus on the man in front of me.

George rests a hand on my waist and leans in. My eyes flutter closed as his lips brush against mine.

Everything fades away. The worry that we'll get caught, the crackle of the fire, and the sounds of the servants outside going about their business. All of it vanishes and becomes obsolete as my world becomes nothing more than George and the way it feels for him to kiss me.

We break apart.

I lift my fingers to my lips, which still tingle with the sensation of our kiss.

"We should sit," I say, finally finding my voice. "I thought we could have some tea."

"That would be delightful, unless you wish for me to leave."

"Leave?" I echo. "Whyever would I wish for that?"

Relief flits over his face, as it becomes clear that he doesn't want to leave. "It is just that I don't want you to think you have to spend more time in my company because we have kissed."

"I would rather think of it as we kissed because I wish to spend more time in your company."

He chuckles. "I wish to think of it that way too."

"Then we shall have tea, converse, and perhaps revisit the kissing part later?" I suggest, picking up the teapot and beginning to make us both a drink. The tea has probably oversteeped, but I do not care.

Not when today has turned out even more wonderful than I'd first imagined.

Chapter 5

DENISE

I glance longingly at the balcony overlooking the dancefloor, disappointed by the group of older ladies who seem to have made it their spot from which to enjoy the festivities. I will have to hope that I can find George somewhere else so that we may spend some time together, or at the very least, arrange another time for him to sneak into the library.

The song comes to an end and I spot Victoria being escorted from the floor by Lord Leon and not looking particularly happy about it. Which is no wonder when she's probably thinking of Viscount Renarton's proposal. She may have said that she didn't believe it was real, but I can tell that it's what she wants.

I turn away, searching the crowd for George even though I know I shouldn't.

I sigh and head towards the refreshments table only to spot Victoria now talking to Mama. She truly has given Lord Leon the slip. I would feel bad for him, but I don't believe he's a good match for her.

Even from this distance, I can see her face crumble. I don't know what happened on the dancefloor, but I'm certain it is not going to be good.

She hurries away from Mama, and I take the opportunity to follow, almost running into Lord Renarton on the way.

He reaches out to steady me, his features lighting up before he realises I'm not Victoria.

"Lord Renarton," I say, curtsying slightly. I suppose I could probably forgo some of the formality given that we've known each other since we were small, and there's a good chance he will become my brother by marriage sooner rather than later, but I err on the side of caution.

"Miss Foxe," he says with a dip of his head. "Have you seen your sister?"

"I saw her head into one of the retiring rooms, I was just about to go and talk to her myself," I say.

Relief flits across his face. I don't know if it is because she is not spending her time with Lord Leon, or because he can assure himself that she is all right. I suppose it is of no matter. He cares, and that is the most important thing.

"Would you tell her that I hope to speak with her?" he asks.

I nod. "Or perhaps you could come to the retiring room just after I go in myself, and you can ask her yourself. I am certain she will prefer your company to mine."

"You believe she will say yes to my proposal?"

"She would be a fool if she did not. I know my sister well, Lord Renarton, and I can plainly see that she cares for you a great deal."

"I am glad I have your approval, Miss Foxe, it means a great deal to me," he says warmly.

I nod. "I will speak with my sister. Follow in a few moments." Asking him to do this is reckless, and could get Victoria into more trouble than she has ever been before, but it feels like the right thing to do.

Lord Renarton nods, and I take it as my cue to leave.

I hurry towards the retiring room I saw my sister enter. "Victoria, it's me. Let me in?"

To my surprise, it only takes a moment for her to pull the door open and let me in. "Did anyone see you come in?"

"No one that didn't see you already. If they don't know we're twins, they probably think they've drunk too much wine and are seeing double."

She laughs nervously.

"Are you all right? I saw you talking with Mama and you seemed distressed."

"No."

I raise an eyebrow, not having expected that answer. "What happened on the dance floor?"

"Lord Leon happened," she admits. "He was giving me all of these instructions about how I would act and dress during our proposal and marriage. And then he went on to talk down to me simply because he deems our family to be beneath his in the shifter hierarchy."

"Oh, Victoria." My heart aches for her. "I have worse news."

She stares at me, the horror clearly etched on her face, but unable to make it through her words.

"I was talking to Miss Priham, she's one of the lioness shifters who were presented last year, and she told me some things about Lord Leon that I think you should know." I gesture for us to sit, knowing she isn't going to like what I have to tell her. Sort of. She'll like the part where Viscount Renarton is right, the rest, I don't believe she will appreciate.

"That doesn't sound good."

"It's not. His family are prominent lion shifters, but they've been struggling to find a good match for him because of his reputation. What the Viscount told you is true, he has multiple mistresses and many illegitimate children. But what he failed to find out was that in not caring for those children, he's brought shame on his family. He's on the verge of being cut off financially by his father, which makes the chance of a good match even less likely." It is horrible to even think of it, but I am glad that we could discover it before she ended up married to him.

"How have we not heard about this before now?" she asks.

"I don't know. The lions are good at keeping quiet about their scandals. Miss Priham only told me because she knew he'd been courting you and wanted to help you save face."

"I'm glad she did. Papa won't stand for our name being linked to a scandal like that."

"No, he won't. You'll be free of him." I reach

out and take her hand in mine, giving it a gentle squeeze. "Don't worry yourself about anything. Stay here and take a moment. I'll deal with telling Mama everything. And if that doesn't work, we'll start the whole ton gossiping about him."

"He can ruin me, though." The desperation in her voice is palpable, and with good reason after Lord Leon caught her alone with the Viscount. She's lucky he hasn't decided to ruin her already. "Won't he just do that in retaliation?"

"I don't think he will. It'll lose his access to your dowry and his respectability. Besides, don't you want to be married to the Viscount?"

"Not like this."

"Ah, so you do." I try not to sound too triumphant, but I don't think it works.

"That's not what I said."

"It isn't what you didn't say either," I counter.

"That's just overcomplicating things."

"So you're trying to tell me you haven't been looking for him all evening to try and talk to him?" It's been obvious to me at every turn, but perhaps she hasn't noticed.

"I want to talk to him," she agrees.

A knock sounds on the door, and relief passes through me.

"Miss Foxe?" the Viscount calls.

"It looks like fate has intervened," I say.

"You told him to come here, didn't you?"

"I shall never admit nor deny the statement." But I'm sure she can already tell the answer.

"Come in," Victoria calls.

The door opens, and the Viscount steps inside, instantly drawing Victoria's full attention. It seems that I am no longer needed.

"Ah, Miss Foxe, I didn't realise you'd be here," he says to me, not doing a particularly good job at pretending.

"I'm just leaving, My Lord." I get to my feet and dip into a curtsy, hurrying away to give them some privacy. I know I shouldn't, but I want Victoria to be happy more than anything, and I think the Viscount can do that.

As much as part of me wants to search for George and assure my own happiness for the rest of the evening, I need to do what I promised and find Mama so I can help with that part of the situation.

I hurry around the ballroom, trying not to worry about how much time is passing. There is a lot of damage Lord Leon could do in such a small amount of time.

"Denise, darling," Mama says, finding me before I can find her.

"Mama, I was looking for you."

"Ah, I'm actually searching for your sister, she seemed upset when she was talking about Lord Leon's proposal."

"I need to tell you about that," I say. "She..." I trail off, spying the subject of our conversation heading towards the retiring room Victoria and the Viscount are currently in.

"Denise? What is it?" Mama asks.

"Victoria is in trouble, we need to go." I gesture towards the retiring room.

Alarm crosses Mama's face, and she hurries in that direction. I follow her, wanting to ensure that my sister is all right.

I let out a small squeak at the sight of the Viscount squaring off against Lord Leon with an angry and determined expression on his face.

Perhaps we never needed to worry about Victoria's well-being in the first place.

"Victoria, what is going on?" Mama says.

I peer past them all to see Victoria looking particularly unsettled.

"Gentlemen, may I have a moment alone with my daughter?" Mama asks.

For a moment, I fear Lord Leon will protest, but he takes himself away.

"It'll be all right," Viscount Renarton promises Victoria. "But I should probably go to the club and find your father as soon as possible." He raises her hand to his lips and kisses it, in a surprisingly intimate gesture given the company.

"I wish you luck."

"I doubt I shall need it, I have my determination," he promises her.

"I'm sorry, Lord Renarton, but I need a moment alone with my daughter," Mama says sternly.

"Of course, Lady Oxinforth, I had no intention of keeping her attention any longer." He bows deeply to her before doing the same to me. "Miss Foxe."

"Close the door," Mama says, instructing me. "Sit down, both of you."

I hurry over, and take a seat by Victoria. She takes my hand in hers and holds it tightly.

"Now the two of you need to tell me what's going on," Mama instructs. "First Victoria is playing her pianoforte far louder than she should, then Denise is allowing you not to call for me, even when you should, and now I learn that you've been caught alone with Lord Renarton. I need some explanations."

I exchange a worried glance with Victoria, but I think we both know there is no way we can keep anything from Mama now.

"Edmund, sorry, the Viscount, may have told Lord Leon that we're already married," Victoria mumbles.

I raise an eyebrow. That's not what I expected.

Mama covers her eyes with her hand and lets out a sigh. "Why would he do that?"

"Lord Leon caught us alone here. Nothing happened," she says hastily. "Well, nothing except me agreeing to his proposal."

"Viscount Renarton proposed to you?" she asks. "When?"

"Yesterday," I say.

Mama switches her attention to me, making me regret speaking. "You knew?"

"Denise was there, Mama. I asked her not to call for you when the Viscount visited because I thought he might want to talk about what happened at Lady Ferrington's ball."

She lets out a small groan. "What happened there?"

"He helped me to fix my hem and Lord Leon

caught us alone." Victoria grimaces. "I know how it sounds, but I promise there was nothing untoward about it."

"If there was nothing untoward, then why does the Viscount wish to marry you?"

"I believe he likes her," I say.

Mama holds up her hand to stop me from speaking. "Don't think that I've forgotten that you knew about this and allowed it to happen. You should have called for me regardless of Victoria's wishes."

"I asked her not to," Victoria says. "And Denise agreed because of Mr Beaumont's visits."

My eyes widen at her plural use of the word. Does she know about the library?

"Visits?" Mama asks. "I am aware of only one." She looks between the two of us.

"Ah, I misspoke," Victoria attempts to fix.

"I wished for a chance to speak with Mr Beaumont privately after we shared a moment at a ball, and Victoria obliged with some rather loud pianoforte."

Mama raises an eyebrow and sighs. "Really, girls? This isn't how I taught you to comport yourselves. But no matter, it seems the situation is already resolved."

"You don't think Papa will say no to Edmund, do you?" Victoria asks, her voice full of nerves.

"When he learned that the heir to the viscounty was the same age as you, he always hoped one of you might be a good match for him. Why do you think the Viscount was invited over so many times as a young boy?" Mama asks.

"Oh."

"So no, I don't think there's going to be a problem with your father. But we have to hope the church will give you a special dispensation to marry, otherwise, we're going to be in a lot of trouble. Hopefully, people can believe we're just trying to keep it quiet to give Denise a chance to find a good match too."

I almost consider saying I've found one, but without her knowing anything about Mr Beaumont, that may not be wise.

"I will get our carriage," Mama says. "It is best if we make ourselves scarce before any rumours start. Wait here and speak to no one." She slips out of the room to do as she says.

I let out a loud sigh. "I'm sorry I couldn't be more help."

"It is not your fault," Victoria assures me. "And I did tell her about Mr Beaumont."

"I know, there was no way around it. But..." I trail off, not wanting to ask her what I know I need to.

"I saw you in the library the other day," she admits. "I didn't see anything, but that was reckless, Denise."

"I know. But I wished to spend time with him, and that was the way I thought of."

"How did you get him inside without anyone noticing?" she asks.

"In my basket."

My sister bursts out laughing. "I hope you realise the thought of that is rather amusing."

"You should try doing it."

"Do you love him?" Victoria asks softly.

"I feel a lot of affection for him. I want to spend time with him, tell him things I've never told anyone before. And when we kiss, it's like nothing else in the world exists."

"You've kissed him? Sister, you've been holding out on me."

"And you on me. The Viscount is telling people you're married now?"

"It isn't like that," she assures me quickly. "I told him I would marry him, we kissed, and then we were caught."

"Mmm."

"I promise, that is all that happened."

"And now you are to be married by the end of the week."

"If Papa says yes," she responds. "And I do not know whether he will."

"Of course he will, you heard Mama. He has wanted this for many years," I assure her.

"Then perhaps this is the perfect time for Mr Beaumont to ask for your hand. If Papa is pleased for my match, then he may be more lenient on yours."

"I suppose only time will tell."

Mama reappears, cutting off our conversation and gesturing for her to follow her out to the carriage and back home.

I can't help but feel disappointed that I won't get to spend any time with George at this ball, but I have hope that Victoria is right and that we'll have a chance to spend even more time together in the future.

Chapter 6

DENISE

As happy as I am for Victoria and her new position as Viscountess Renarton, I'm also starting to truly despise the effect it has had on me. Mama has made me go to even more social engagements than before, and is keeping a closer watch on me now that she realises I've been left to my own devices a little too much.

But with every dance and conversation with a gentleman who *isn't* George Beaumont, I become more and more certain that he's the person I want to be spending the time with.

The current set ends, causing a flurry of dancers to leave the floor.

Unfortunately, it also means that a bevy of gentlemen approach me, each of them vying for the next dance. This is the problem with being the daughter of a baron and the sister of a viscountess. I have become rather desirable to the single gentlemen of the ton.

And yet I do not want any of them.

I search among the faces, spying Victoria and the Viscount further away. For a moment, I hope Lord Renarton might come to save me from the masses and dance with me. I am sure Victoria would not mind.

"Miss Foxe."

The familiar voice sends a thrill of excitement through me, along with relief.

I turn to find George by me.

He dips into a low bow. "Might I have this dance, Miss Foxe?"

"It would be my pleasure, Mr Beaumont."

He holds out his hand and I slip mine into it, feeling a small thrill as his fingers close around mine.

There's a small grumble from the assembled gentlemen, but none of them know me well enough to really mind. Nor do they particularly care.

George draws me out onto the floor to take our place in one of the lower set. It doesn't escape my notice that he places us in a position where we will not be required to dance for a while, allowing us some time to converse while the other couples do their part of the dance.

The music starts, and the couple at the top of our set begin to move through their steps.

"Thank you for saving me," I say. "Though I would much rather be on the balcony than here."

He chuckles. "I would prefer the same, but since your sister's marriage, it seems as if your mother is keeping a closer eye on you than ever before."

"You would not be wrong about that. Is there any scandal about my sister?"

"None that I have heard. Should there be?"

"Only that the Viscount loves her very much," I respond.

"Ah, so we are not the only ones who have flirted with the rules."

"Mr Beaumont," I warn. "This is not the place."

"My apologies, Miss Foxe."

"No, it is me who should apologise. The last few weeks have been exhausting. Mama has been pressuring me to go to all these events, and has been watching to ensure that I actually interact with the gentlemen there, when all I really wish is to be sat on the balcony with you."

The couple ahead of us come to a stand-

The Lady and the Rabbit

still, and it is our turn to dance, cutting into our conversation. Though I am not worried about that. After so many clandestine meetings, I am certain that our conversation will be picked up the moment we are standing still again.

My hand brushes against George's as we turn in the dance, bringing us close together, but not close enough for my liking.

Even so, I have to admit that there is a joy in being able to dance with him that I didn't expect to feel. Perhaps it is simply about the public declaration of interest. No one will think twice about it unless we dance again. But it is enough for me.

We spin around one final time and come to a rest until we're needed for the set once more.

"I thought you could not dance," I say.

"I never said that I could not, just that I did not enjoy it."

"Oh." I watch the other dancers. "I did not mean for you to do something you do not like."

George chuckles. "It is not that I do not like dancing, it is the meaningless conversation of which I am not a fan."

"Ah."

"And with you, I certainly don't get that."

My heart skips a beat, even though I know what he's saying is true.

We take a few more turns as the dance requires, until the set finally comes to an end.

"Would you like me to escort you to the refreshments, Miss Foxe?" George asks.

"That would be lovely, Mr Beaumont." I slip my arm through his, resting my hand on the sleeve of his jacket.

He leads me away from the dancefloor and towards where the refreshment stands are, though it doesn't escape my notice that he is taking a longer route than he needs to.

"The last few social events have been rather unpleasant without my companion to discuss them with," he admits.

"I must apologise for that."

"You should not. We both knew what we were doing was reckless, and that there was a chance that we would not be able to at some point," he says. "But as soon as I realised how much I missed you, I knew I had to say one thing to you."

"And that is?" Hope wells up in my chest.

"I know we are of different stations, and that my means are much less than some of these other suitors who are interested in your hand, but I would ask you to marry me in an instant if I thought you would say yes."

"But George, I would say yes."

He turns to face me, his gaze full of hope. "You would?"

I nod. "Of course. I search for you at every ball. And try to get away to find somewhere safe to hide from the rest of the people here. I want to live a life with you. And I do not care that you don't have a title, or that you aren't of as high an income as other potential suitors. Because you have something that they do not."

"Good sense?"

I let out a small laugh. "I was going to say my heart, but your guess may also be correct."

"And you have mine, Denise." He takes a deep breath. "But this is not me asking you to marry me."

"Oh?"

"I wish to do it properly."

"Which means you'll need to speak with my father."

"Precisely."

"In which case, we should head in this direction and I shall introduce you properly to my sister and the Viscount," I say, leading him away from the refreshments and to where I can see the two of them talking.

"I am not sure how that will help me with your father," he says.

"Because the Viscount has recently had the experience of asking him for permission to marry Victoria, and in a situation much more precarious than ours." Though from the things Victoria has told me, the two of them spent much less time alone than we have.

"Then introduce away," he says. "And then perhaps we may find a place to spend a private moment?"

"I would like that very much," I say, meaning every word and feeling as if I'm floating.

I know there is still much that can go wrong before we can wed, but tonight feels as if it is the start of something new.

Chapter 7

GEORGE

I stop outside the door to the club, trying not to feel too nervous about being a new member and needing to speak with someone who had held his membership for several decades. But Viscount Renarton said that this was the best place to speak to Baron Oxinforth, so this is where I shall do it.

And it helps that the Viscount informed me he'll be visiting himself today. I may not know the man well, but Denise has spoken highly of him, and from our limited interactions, he seems like a good man.

I make my way inside, nodding to the footmen on the door while half expecting them to stop me from going any further.

Nervousness is my constant companion as I climb the steps.

"Ah, Beaumont," Viscount Renarton says as I enter the room. He gets to his feet and heads in my direction. "I was just about to have a drink with the Baron, why don't you join us?"

"Are you sure he'll find that acceptable?" I ask.

The Viscount chuckles. "I requested his presence by saying there was something important I wished to discuss with him," he says. "I'm sure he probably believes I wish to tell him that Lady Renarton is with child, but he will like this better."

I let out an amused laugh. "You don't believe that he would like grandchildren?"

"I think he would dislike it considering the short time we have been married. It would almost make it seem as if my wife was with child before the wedding, which I can assure you was not the case."

He draws me through to a private room and gestures for a servant to bring us some drinks.

"I hope I do not disappoint him with the subject of the conversation," I say.

"Miss Foxe would not have suggested you talk to him if she didn't believe you had a reasonable chance of securing his favour," the Viscount says. "Everyone believes that my wife is the more headstrong of the two of them, but that is because they have not been on the receiving end of Miss Foxe's determination."

"I shall keep that in mind." I take a seat next to the Viscount while the two of us wait for the Baron to arrive.

Our drinks appear, and I nod in thanks to the servant and pick up the glass, mostly for something to do with my hands while the nervous energy consumes me.

It isn't until the Baron walks into the room that I finally realise I have somewhere to direct it.

I've never seen him before, but I can see the resemblance to his daughters in the shape of his face.

"Renarton," he says, clapping a hand on the younger man's shoulder. "Always a pleasure. How is my daughter?"

"She is well, My Lord," he responds.

"Excellent. And who is this?" He seems more intrigued than annoyed, which is a good sign. Or I hope it is.

"This is Mr Beaumont," Renarton introduces. "He wishes to speak with you."

The Baron raises an eyebrow, but takes a seat regardless. "Beaumont, you say?" he checks.

"Yes, My Lord," I respond, my mouth suddenly dry. I've been prepared for many things in my life, but asking for Denise's hand in marriage isn't one of them.

"Any relation to the Earl who shares your name?"

"I'm from a distant branch of the family. The chances of my inheriting are very slim," I admit, not seeing any point in embellishing the truth. "My family's money comes from shipping."

"Interesting, that is not an avenue I have explored to expand the Barony. Is that why you wished to introduce us, Renarton?"

"It is not," the Viscount responds. "Mr Beaumont has been courting Denise." The familiarity of the way he refers to her isn't lost on either of us. Which makes sense to me. While the Viscount and Denise refer to one another formally when they speak, it does not change the fact they have known one another since childhood.

The Baron raises an eyebrow. "I had not realised my daughter was courting anyone."

Ah, that is a problem we didn't think about. "We've been taking our time to get to know one another, My Lord," I say.

The Baron nods. "And am I to assume that your

visit today means that you wish to ask for my permission to marry her?"

"I do."

The Baron nods. "I see."

I wait, not wanting to rush him despite my impatience to tell me whether or not I have his permission to ask.

"Why do you wish to marry my daughter?" the Baron asks.

"Why?"

"It is a simple question, Beaumont."

I take a deep breath, trying to articulate my thoughts, even when it is hard to. "Because I care deeply for her. She is intelligent and well-read, with a quick wit and keen observational skills."

"So it is nothing to do with her sizable dowry?"

I blink a few times. "I was not aware of that. She never said anything about it."

The Viscount clears his throat. "The Viscountess says that they have been courting since before the dowry increase."

To my surprise, the Baron lets out an amused chuckle. "My daughters have been keeping things from me." He doesn't seem too angry about that. "Very well. If Denise approves, then I would be a poor father to deny her what her heart wishes for."

"I have your permission to ask her to marry me?"

"You do," he responds. "But should she say no, that will be the end of it."

"Thank you, Your Lordship." Relief crashes through me as I realise that this is going to end the way I want it to.

Now all I have to do is formally ask Denise to be my wife.

Chapter 8

DENISE

I pace back and forth, trying to calm the anxiousness building inside me.

"You should sit," Victoria says, gesturing to the chaise by her.

"I can't sit. Would you be able to sit if you were waiting for the Viscount to gain permission to marry you?"

"You're forgetting that I did have to sit and wait. And that it was worse considering everyone already thought we were married," she points out.

"That isn't helpful."

"Papa isn't going to say no, Denise," she says instead. "Why would he? Unless you've completely misjudged Mr Beaumont and he's after your fortune."

"I feel like he could have made wiser choices if it was money he was after."

"I agree. There are several wealthy heiresses who are currently available, I believe one of them would be a more suitable target for fortune hunters, which means that you have nothing to worry about."

"You're not helping." I sit down beside her.

Victoria reaches out and takes my hand in hers. "He will. He wouldn't have asked Edmund for his help otherwise. Making an enemy of a viscount isn't the wisest decision to make."

"That was almost helpful."

"Then it's an improvement," she responds brightly.

The double doors open and Varley steps in. "Mr Beaumont to see Miss Foxe."

My heart skips a beat and I glance at my sister, who just smiles happily at me as if she knows what this means and how important it is.

"Do I sit?" I ask her. "Or is it better to stand?"

"I think that is your choice," she responds, sounding bemused.

The moment George steps through the door, I stand up and hurry over to him.

"How did it go? What did he say?" I ask, trying not to get too ahead of myself.

"It went well," he says, gazing at me with a lot of affection in his eyes.

Victoria rises to her feet. "I promised the Viscount I would ask the cook for more lemon biscuits," she says. "Ours can't make them correctly, apparently."

I glance at my sister, curious about why she announced such a mundane thing to the room.

"Mama is in the gardens, I don't wish to walk past her until you've had your moment alone," she explains.

"Thank you."

The way she smiles shows me just how happy she is for me. Even so, I'm glad she's decided to leave the room.

"Shall we sit?" George asks.

"That depends, are we trying to make it so that my parents have no option but to agree to a wedding?"

He chuckles. "There's no need to force anything," he promises.

"Papa said yes?"

"He said he would approve so long as you did.

Though I suspect in part we have the Viscount to thank for that."

"It can be his penance for ruining my favourite ribbon," I jest. "Though I suppose I should have forgiven him for that as a wedding present."

George leads me over to the chaise and we sit.

"I know you have already expressed your desires on the matter, but I have to ask. Denise Foxe, will you do me the great honour of becoming my wife?"

My heart soars just hearing the words. "Nothing would make me happier. A thousand times, yes."

He reaches out and tucks a stray lock of hair behind my ear. "I love you, Denise."

"I love you too." I slide myself closer to him, not seeing the harm considering we're already alone and Papa has agreed to our wedding.

"When do you think we'll be able to get married," I ask.

"As soon as possible without raising suspicions."

"Or the cost. I don't believe we have the same resources available to use as the Viscount did for his wedding to Victoria," I say.

"I don't know whether to be disappointed that we don't have to pretend to already be married like they did, or if I'm pleased that I can escort you to some events as my betrothed first," he says.

"The latter will aid me in avoiding the overeager gentlemen who wish only to court me for my connection to my sister," I muse. "Though it may be harder for us to have moments to ourselves."

"Other than this one?" he asks.

An amused laugh escapes me. "Mama isn't here because she believes Victoria is."

"Then we shall just have to ask your sister to act as a chaperone more often."

"That is true. When she's our chaperone, I can do this." I lean in and press my lips against his.

He responds to my kiss instantly, slipping an arm around my waist and pulling me closer. His touch is tender and loving, leaving me with no apprehension about whether he wants to go ahead with this wedding.

I break the kiss, a joyful smile spreading over my face.

"Even if Victoria doesn't chaperone, there's another way we can spend time together and not get caught," I say.

"Oh?"

"It all depends on whether you like my basket or not."

He lets out an amused laugh. "A journey in the basket ends with time spent with you, to me, that is worth it even if I did not like the basket. Though that does remind me that I have never seen you in your shifted form."

I frown, not having thought about that. "I hadn't realised. We should change that at some point, though I do not spend much time in it."

"I have spent more in mine in the past few weeks than I have in the past few years. There is never much call for rabbit shifters."

"There should be."

"I am content in the knowledge that you like my shifted form," he responds.

"I do," I promise. "And I look forward to seeing it many more times in our life together, even if there are no baskets involved."

"I would hop into any basket for you," he promises.

I smile and lean in to kiss him again, content in the knowledge that I'll soon be able to call myself his wife.

Thank you for reading *The Lady and the Rabbit*, I hope you enjoyed it! If you would like to read more from *The Shifter Season* series, you can start with Victoria's story in *The Fox and the Viscount*: https://books.authorlauragreenwood.co.uk/theladyandtherabbit

Author Note

Thank you for reading *The Lady and the Rabbit*, I hope you enjoyed it!

I know a lot of people have been waiting for this story since the release of *The Fox and the Viscount*, which follows Denise's twin, Victoria, and I want to thank you for your patience while I worked on it. I hope you enjoyed it!

If you want to keep up to date with new releases and other news, you can join my Facebook Reader Group or mailing list.

Stay safe & happy reading!

- Laura

Also by Laura Greenwood

You can find out more about each of my series on my website.

- Obscure Academy: a paranormal romance series set at a university-age academy for mixed supernaturals. Each book follows a different couple.
- The Apprentice Of Anubis: an urban fantasy series set in an alternative world where the Ancient Egyptian Empire never fell. It follows a new apprentice to the temple of Anubis as she learns about her new role.
- Forgotten Gods: a paranormal adventure romance series inspired by Egyptian mythology. Each book follows a different Ancient Egyptian goddess.
- Amethyst's Wand Shop Mysteries (with Arizona Tape): an urban fantasy murder mystery series following a witch who teams up with a detective to solve murders. Each book includes a different murder.
- Grimm Academy: a fantasy fairy tale academy series. Each book follows a different fairy tale heroine.

- Jinx Paranormal Dating Agency: a paranormal romance series based on worldwide mythology where paranormals and deities take part in events organised by the Jinx Dating Agency. Each book follows a different couple.
- Purple Oasis (with Arizona Tape): a paranormal romance series based at a sanctuary set up after the apocalypse. Each book follows a different couple.
- Speed Dating With The Denizens Of The Underworld (shared world): a paranormal romance shared world based on mythology from around the world. Each book follows a different couple.
- Blackthorn Academy For Supernaturals (shared world): a paranormal monster romance shared world based at Blackthorn Academy. Each book follows a different couple.

You can find a complete list of all my books on my website:

https://books.authorlauragreenwood.co.uk/book-list

Signed Paperback & Merchandise:

You can find signed paperbacks, hardcovers, and

merchandise based on my series (including stickers, magnets, face masks, and more!) via my website:

https://books.authorlauragreenwood.co.uk/shop

About Laura Greenwood

Laura is a USA Today Bestselling Author of paranormal romance, urban fantasy, and fantasy romance. When she's not writing, she drinks a lot of tea, tries to resist French macarons, and works towards a diploma in Egyptology. She lives in the UK, where most of her books are set. Laura specialises in quick reads, with healthy relationships and consent-positive moments regardless of if she's writing light-hearted romance, mythology-heavy urban fantasy, or anything in between.

Follow Laura Greenwood

- Website: www.authorlaura-greenwood.co.uk
- Mailing List: https://books.authorlauragreenwood.co.uk/newsletter
- Facebook Group: http://facebook.com/groups/theparanormalcouncil
- Facebook Page: http://facebook.com/authorlauragreenwood

- Bookbub: https://www.bookbub.com/authors/laura-greenwood

Printed in Great Britain
by Amazon